The Pilgrimage of Charlemagne

Anonymous

MythBank

This edition is Copyright © 2020 by Jason Hamilton

All rights reserved.

No original part of this book may be reproduced in any form or by any electronic or mechanical means, including information storage and retrieval systems, without written permission from the author. All short stories found therein are in the public domain.

Arthurian Legends

www.arthurlegends.com

MythBank

www.mythbank.com

Cover design by Jason Hamilton.

Contents

About MythBank	v
1. The Dialogue of Myrddin and Taliesin	1
2. Meigant	4
3. God Supreme	6
4. The Ode to Cyridwen	9
5. A Skillful Composition	11
6. Soul, Since I Was Made	14
7. Let Us Not Reproach	15
8. The Triads of the Horses	17
9. Let God Be Praised	19
10. Hail, Glorious Lord	22
11. I Will Extol Thee	24
12. In the Name of the Lord	26
13. There Is A Graciously Disposed King	28
14. Tenby	32
15. Dinas Maon	36
16. The Birch Trees	37

17. The Apple Trees	39
18. Listen, Piglet	44
19. The Stanzas of the Graves	52
20. The Cynghogion of Elaeth	64
21. Not To Call Upon God	66
22. Gereint son of Erbin	68
23. Duv in kymhorth	72
24. Assuynaw naut duv diamehv	75
25. As Long As We Sojourn	78
26. The First Song of Yscolan	79
27. The Second Song of Yscolan	81
28. Gvledic ar bennic erbin attad	85
29. A Blessing To the Happy Youth	87
30. Keen the Gale	89
31. Arthur and the Porter	96
32. A Song on Gwallawg ab Llenawg	101
33. The Dialogue of Gwyn ap Nudd and Gwyddno Garahir	103
34. Though I Love the Strand	107
35. The Dialogue of Taliesin and Ugnach	109
36. Marunad Madawc mad Maredut	112
37. Marunad Madawc fil Maredut	114
38. Seithenhin	117
39. The Names of the Sons of Llywarch Hen	119
More Celtic Legends	122

About MythBank

MythBank is a website devoted to the documentation and study of stories. As part of that initiative, this collection was created with the purpose of ensuring all public domain classics had attractive, uniform, and readily available print copies and ebooks.

Through print on demand, many classics that are lesser-known or have limited runs can still be available for anyone who wants it, keeping the price steady and reducing the need to search the dregs of used books for a copy that might cost ten times what it's worth.

We hope you enjoy this collection of classics and recommend you visit our website to learn more. Additionally, you will find other classics in this collection that are designed to match the same branding and tone of this volume, so they look amazing on your shelf or your device. Check them out!

The Dialogue of Myrddin and Taliesin

MYRDDIN:
How sad with me, how said,
Cedfyl and Cadfan are fallen!
The slaughter was terrible,
Shields shattered and bloody.

Taliesin:
I saw Maelgwn battling--
The host acclaimed him.

Myrddin:
Before two men in battles they gather
Before Erith and Gwrith on pale horses.
Slender bay mounts will they bring
Soon will come the host of Elgan.
Alas for his death, after a great joy!

Taliesin:

Gap-toothed Rhys, his shield a span--

To him came battle's blessing.

Cyndur has fallen, deplorable beyond measure

Generous men have been slain--

Three notable men, greatly esteemed by Elgan.

Myrddin:

Again and again, in great throngs they came,

There came Bran and Melgan to meet me.

At the last, they slew Dyel,

The son of Erbin, with all his men.

Taliesin:

Swifly came Maelgwn's men,

Warriors ready for battle, for slaughter armed.

For this battle, Arderydd, they have made

A lifetime of preparation.

Myrddin:

A host of spears fly high, drawing blood.

From a host of vigorous warriors--

A host, fleeing; a host, wounded--

A host, bloody, retreating.

Taliesin:

The seven sons of Eilfer, seven heroes,

Will fail to avoid seven spears in the battle.

Myrddin:

Seven fires, seven armies,

Cynelyn in every seventh place.

Taliesin:

Seven spears, seven rivers of blood

From seven chieftains, fallen.

Myrddin:

Seven score heroes, maddened by battle,

To the forest of Celyddon they fled.

Since I Myrddin, am second only to Taliesin,

Let my words be heard as truth.

Meigant

A DREAM I HAPPEN TO see last night; clever is he that can interpret it.

It shall not be related to the wanton; he that will not conceal it shall know it not.

It is an act of the gentle to govern the multitude. Pleasure is not the wealth of a country.

Have I not been under the same covering with a fair maid of the hue of the billow of the strand?

Labour bestowed on anything good is no pain, and the remembrance of it will last.

Worse is my trouble to answer him who is not acquainted with it.

It is no reparation for an evil deed, a desistence after it is done.

One's benefit does not appear when it is asked for in a roundabout way: thou hadst better keep to what there is.

And associate with the virtuous, and be resolute as to what may happen.

He that frequently commits crime will at last be caught.

He that will not relate a thing fully, will not find himself contradicted.

Riches will not flourish with the wicked. Mass will not be sung on a retreat.

A sigh is no protection against the vile. He that is not liberal does not deserve the name.

God Supreme

GOD SUPREME, BE MINE the Awen! Amen; fiat!

A successful song of fruitful praise, relating to the bustling course of the host,

According to the sacred ode of Cyridwen, the goddess of various seeds,

The various seeds of poetic harmony, the exalted speech of the graduated minstrel,

Cuhelyn the bard of elegant Cymraec utterly rejects.

A poem for a favour, the gift of friendship, will not be maintained.

But a composition of thorough praise is being brought to thee,

Splendid singer in a choir, and of a song equal in length and motion.

Appropriate and full were the tuneful horns, gloriously ascended the conflagration

Of the nation of the border, whose troops were of the same pace and simultaneous movement.

Praise the hero, whose gift is large, the benefit of humble suitors.

Light is the rebuke of the rallying-point of relatives, the winner of praise,

A skilful fastener, for a hundred calends, the accumulator of heat;

A fierce frowning wolf, whose inflexible disposition is law, accustomed to jurisdiction.

Eidoel was a man extremely brave, very choice and full of wisdom

A leader as regards the Brython, full of knowledge and prudence, fiery in his wrath;

Accustomed to hatred, accustomed to harmony, and to the high seat in the banquet of mead;

Partaker of the intoxicating wine, a knight of the list, a place of limitation;

A lord who is the measurer of the wall, the delight of the four quarters, the great centre power;

A knight of stout conduct, a knight of virtuous conduct, with warriors full of rage;

A guardian celebrated in song, a fine panegyric, the blandishment of language.

Odious was his death by Nognaw. Am I not agitated? The active and eloquent one will I praise;

A contented ruler, a restless guardian, energetic and wise. A company of active reapers, melodious poetry, and the assuaging of wrath;

A talented hero, like a furious wave over the strand,

The marrow of fine songs, a contemplative mind, a sacred mystery;

A servitor with knowledge, the possession of mead, an agreeable eulogy;

Music which has melody like that of a golden organ, a place of retirement;

rhe action of law against violence, the admirable vigour of the brave, the energy of the Supreme Being.

A blessing I will venture to ask, a blessing I will pray for, I will bind myself thereby;

The wonderful rush of the gale, the pervasion of fire, the war of youth;

One deserving of ruddy gold, one liberal of praise furrowed (with age), a free wing;

Ready affluence, a rill in a pleasant shelter, a reward for a panegyric.

The most deserving will yield, he will keep his refuge from the insult of the enemy:

He has completely kept the law, completely shown his disposition before the placid Ogyrven.

For a good turn from me, may the gift of Cuhelyn give satisfaction of mind.

The Ode to Cyridwen

ACCORDING TO THE SACRED ode of Cyridwen, the Ogyrven of various seeds,—

The various seeds of poetic harmony, the exalted speech of the graduated minstrel,

Cuhelyn the wise, of elegant Cymraec, an exalted possession,

Will skilfully sing; the right of Aedan, the lion, shall be heard.

A song of fulness, worthy of a chair, a powerful composition it is.

From suitors may he receive eulogy, and they presents from him

The bond of sovereigns, the subject of contests in harmonious song.

Splendid are his horses, hundreds respect him, the skilful seek the chieftain,

The circle of deliverance, the nation's refuge, and a treasure of mutual reproach.

To banter with him, who is of a venerable form, I would devoutly desire;

A broad defence, like a ship to the suppliant, and a port to the minstrel,

Quick as lightning, a powerful native, a chief whose might is sharp;

A luminary of sense, much he knows, completely lie accomplishes.

May the hero of the banquet, through peace, enforce tranquillity from this day.

A Skillful Composition

A SKILLFUL COMPOSITION, THE PATTERN being from God,

A composition, the language, beautiful and pleasant, from Christ.

And should there be a language all complete around the sun,

On as many pivots as there are under the seat,

On as many winged ones as the Almighty made,

And should every one have thrice three hundred tongues,

They could not relate the power of the Trinity.

A diligent man in prosperity will receive no punishment.

Let communion be ready against the Trinity.

Let him be ill and ailing when is flesh becomes weak,

That he may puff his disguise.

Woe to thee, man of passion; if the world were given me,

Unless thou wert to deliver thyself, thou wouldst be satiated of the evil.

Art thou not at liberty as regards what thy mind loves?

Furious thy violent death, thy being borne on the wattled frame;

More wretched thy end, thy interment in the grave,

And being trodden by feet in the midst of soil and sod.

Unequalled thy journey, thy separation from thy companions.

Faithless and useless body, think of thy soul!

Body, thou wouldst not hear when others spoke.

What gayest thou of thy wealth before private confession?

What gayest thou of thy riches before the close and silent pit?

And what thou hadst intended, thou hast left undone;

And thou sawest not how many thou shouldst have loved.

And a benefit it would have been as regards the passions of the people.

And the good would have come to so much prosperity.

When thou of thy freedom purchasest a hundred things, they are uncertain,

And vanish as suddenly as the motion of eyelid.

Hast thou noticed that they love sinisterly while seeking violence?

Thou respectedst not Friday, of thy great humility;

Thou chantedst not a *paternoster* at matins or vespers,

A paternoster, the chief thing to be repeated: meditate on nothing

Except the Trinity.

Thou shouldst pay what is equal to three seven paternosters daily.

What has been and is not, and their life has not passed away.

Thou art more accustomed to the roaring of the sea than to the preaching of the evangel

Must thou not go to the pile, because thou hast not been humble?

Thou respectedst neither relics, nor altars, nor churches.

Thou didst not attend to the strains of bards of harmonious utterance.

Thou didst not respect the law of the Creator of heaven before death.

A strange mixture didst thou employ in thy speech.

Woe is me that I went with thee to our joint work!

Woe is me when I am about to praise thee!

When I came to thee, small was my evil,

But it came to me from thy grovelling co-operation.

As for them, none will believe us respecting thy appearance of enjoyment.

Soul, Since I Was Made

SOUL, SINCE I WAS made in necessity blameless

True it is, woe is me that thou shouldst have come to my design,

Neither for my own sake, nor for death, nor for end, nor for beginning.

It was with seven faculties that I was thus blessed,

With seven created beings I was placed for purification;

I was gleaming fire when I was caused to exist;

I was dust of the earth, and grief could not reach me;

I was a high wind, being less evil than good;

I was a mist on a mountain seeking supplies of stags;

I was blossoms of trees on the face of the earth.

If the Lord had blessed me, He would have placed me on matter.

Soul, since I was made -

Let Us Not Reproach

LET US NOT REPROACH one another, but rather mutually save ourselves.

Certain is a meeting after separation,

The appointment of a senate, and a certain conference,

And the rising from the grave after a long repose.

The mighty God will keep in his power the man of correct life,

And will let fire upon the unholy people,

And lightning and thunder and wide-spread death.

Neither a solitary nor a sluggard shall pass to a place of safety.

And after peace there shall be the usages of a kingdom;

The three hosts shall be brought to the overpowering presence of Jesus:

A pure and blessed host like the angels;

Another host, mixed, like the people of a country;

The third host, unbaptized, a multitude that directly after death

Will proceed in a thick crowd to the side of devils,

Not one of them shall go, owing to their hideous forms,

To the place where there are flowers and dew on the pleasant land,

Where there are singers tuning their harmonious lays,

Happy will be their cogitations with the ruler of the glorious retinue;

Where the Apostles are in the kingdom of the humble,

Where the bounteous Creator is on his glorious throne.

May a disposition for the grave be given us; exalted is a relationship to Him;

And before we are gathered together to mount Olivet,

May those who have fallen be victorious over death;

And work like theirs may we also do; for at the judgment day

The wonders, greatness, and puissance of the Creator none can relate.

The Triads of the Horses

THE THREE DEPREDATORY HORSES of the Isle of Prydain

Carnawlawg, the horse of Owain the son of Urien;

Bucheslwm Seri, the horse of Gwgawn Gleddyvrudd;

And Tavawd Mr Breich-hir, the horse of Cadwallawn the son of Cadvan.

The three draught-horses of the Isle of Prydain

Arvul Melyn, the horse of Pasgen the son of Urien; -

Du Hir Terwenydd, the horse of Selyv the son of Cynan Garwyn;

And Drudlwyd, the horse of Rhydderch Hael.

The three spirited horses of the Isle of Prydain

Gwineu Goddwf Hir, the horse of Cai;

Rhuthr Eon Tuth Blaidd, the horse of Gilbert the son of Cadgyffro;

And Ceincaled, the horse of Gwalchmai.

The three high-mettled horses of the Isle of Prydain

Lluagor, the horse of Carndawg;

And Melynlas, the horse of Caswallawn the son of Bei.

(Possibly forgotten is Melyngar Mangre, the horse of Lleu Llaw Gyffes)

Let God Be Praised

LET GOD BE PRAISED in the beginning and the end.

Who supplicates Him, He will neither despise nor refuse.

The only son of Mary, the great exemplar of kings,

Mary, the mother of Christ, the praise of women.

The sun will come from the East to the North.

Intercede, for thy great mercy's sake,

With thy Son, the glorious object of our love,

God above us, God before us, God possessing (all things).

May the Father of Heaven grant us a portion of mercy;

Puissant Sovereign, may there be peace between us without refusal;

May we reform and make satisfaction for our transgressions,

Before I go to the earth to my fresh grave,

In the dark without a candle to my tribunal,

To my narrow abode, to the limits assigned to me, to my repose;

After my horse, and indulgence in fresh mead,

And social feasting, and gallantry with women.

I will not sleep; I will meditate on my end.

We are in a state the wantonness of which is sad;

Like leaves from the top of trees it will vanish away.

Woe to the niggard that hoards up precious things;

And unless the Supreme Father will support him,

Though he is allowed to have his course in the present world, his end will be dangerous.

He knows not what it is to be brave, yet will he not tremble in his present state;

He will not rise up in the morning, will utter no greeting, nor will he sit;

He will not sing joyfully nor ask for mercy.

Bitter will, in the end, be the retribution

Of haughtiness, arrogance, and restlessness.

He pampers his body for toads and snakes

And lions, and conceives iniquity.

And death will come upon hoary age;

He is insatiable in the assembly and in the banquet.

Old age will draw nigh, and spreads itself over thee.

Thy ear, thy sight, thy teeth, they will not return;

The skin of thy fingers will wrinkle,

And age and hoariness will affect thee.

May Michael make intercession for us, that the Father of heaven may dispense us His mercy!

The beginning of summer is a most pleasant season, tuneful the birds, green the stalks of plants,

Ploughs are in the furrow, oxen in the yoke,

Green is the sea, variegated the land.

When cuckoos sing on the branches of pleasant trees,

LET GOD BE PRAISED 21

May my joyfulness become greater.

Smoke is painful, sleeplessness is manifest.

Since my friends are returned to their former state

In the hill, in the dale, in the islands of the sea,

In every direction that one goes, in the presence of the blessed Christ there is no terror.

It was our desire, our friend, our trespass

To penetrate into the land of thy banishment.

Seven saints and seven score and seven hundred did he pierce in one convention.

With Christ the blessed they sustain no apprehension of evil.

A gift I will ask, may it not be refused me by the God of peace.

Since there is a way to the gate of the Supreme Father,

Christ, may I not be sad before thy throne!

Hail, Glorious Lord

HAIL, GLORIOUS LORD!
May church and chancel bless Thee

And chancel and church

And plain and precipice!

And the three fountains there are,

Two above wind, and one above the earth.

May darkness and light bless Thee I

And fine silk and sweet trees!

Abraham the chief of faith did bless Thee.

And life eternal.

And birds and bees.

And old and young.

Aaron and Moses did bless Thee.

And male and female.

And the seven days and the stars.

And the air and the ether.

And books and letters.

And llsh in the flowing water.

And song and deed.

And sand and sward.

And such as were satisfied with good.

I will bless Thee, glorious Lord!

Hail, glorious Lord!

I Will Extol Thee

I.

I WILL EXTOL THEE, THE Trinity in the mysterious One,

Who is One and Three, a Unity of one energy,

Of the same essence and attributes, one God to be praised.

I will praise Thee, great Father, whose mighty works are great;

To praise Thee is just; to praise Thee is incumbent on me.

The produce of poetry is the right of Eloi.

Hail, glorious Christ!

Father, and Son, and Spirit! Lord,

God, Adonai!

II.

I will extol God, who is both One and Two,

Who is Three without any error, without its being easily doubted;

Who made fruit, and nil, and every gushing stream;

God is his name, being two Divine Ones to be cornprehended;

God is his name, being three Divine Ones in his energy;

God is his name, being One; the God of Paul and Anhun.

III.

I will extol One, who is both Two and One.

Who is, besides, Three, who is God Himself,

Who made Mars and Luna, and male and female,

And ordained that the shallow and the abyss should not be of equal depth;

Who made heat and cold, and sun and moon,

And letters in the wax, and flame in the candle,

And affection to be one of the senses, and lovely woman late,

And caused the burning of five Caers, and an erring consort.

In the Name of the Lord

IN THE NAME OF the Lord, mine to adore, whose praise is great.

I will praise the great Ruler, whose blessing is great on an almsdeed;

The God that defends us, the God that made us, the God that will deliver us,

The God of our hope, blessed, perfect, and pure is his true happiness.

God owns us; God is above, the Triune King,

God has been felt a support to us in affliction;

God has been, by being imprisoned, in humility.

May the blessed Ruler make us free against the day of doom,

And bring us to the feast, for the sake of his meekness and lowliness,

And happily receive us into Paradise from the burden of sin,

And give us salvation, for the sake of his agony and five wounds,

Terrible anguish God delivered us when he assumed flesh.

Man would have been lost, had He not ransomed him, according to his glorious ordinance.

From the bloody Cross came redemption to the whole world.

Christ the mighty Shepherd, his merits will never fail.

There Is A Graciously Disposed King

THERE IS A GRACIOUSLY disposed King, who is wonderful in the highest degree,

Who is chief above the children of Adam,

Who is a happy and most mighty defence [sic],

Who is generous, glorious, and most pure,

Whose claim is most strong and binding.

What is heard of him, and what is true, that will I celebrate. I

To the great God, to the condescending and most compassionate God,

To the blessed God a sacred song I will sing.

Until I become a blameless man to God, I will consider the substance,

About the sin which Adam sinned.

About sin before the judgment I am very anxious,

Against the day of appointment, when all men shall come

From their graves in their strength and greatest vigour,

As they were when they were in their very prime,

In one host to the one place most pleasant,

Even to the top of one hill, in order to be judged.

THERE IS A GRACIOUSLY DISPOSED KING

Among this multitude may I attain the merit

Of being protected by a retinue of the nine orders of Heaven.

My God! what a gathering!

My Lord God! may my bardic lore

Affect the bonds of the universe!

My great Superior! my Owner!

The object of my reverence! before going to the sod, before going to the gravel,

Permit thou me to indite a composition

To thy praise, before my tongue becomes mute,

And my memory like Job, who spoke

Unto his wife concerning her dragonic obedience.

When the servant of God on a certain day came

To him to the contest with his wife,

Before the blow he gave a handful

Of what had peeled from the surface of his flesh.

And since the presents which any one gave were now acceptable,

The merciful God made a gift of charity

In pure gold, the treasure of the Trinity.

In a fainting state he sits, and there praises God.

Blessed was he to be plagued! Now said Sin,

'Thou knowest how to conceal the perfidy of the mysterious Being."

The love-diffusing Lord of heaven, the Creator, take thou to praise Him,

That thou mayest reach the fair and happy region,

Happy, pleasant, free, and greatly deserving praise.

Loving wine, love thou. the gentle, preserve the truth.

Eva did not preserve the sweet apple-tree which God commanded her.

For her transgression He was not reconciled to her,

But manifest pain he inflicted upon her.

Some wonderful covering of a flinty dress she put on herself;

The Maker of heaven caused her, in the midst of her riches, to make herself bare.

And a second miracle did the bountiful Lord, who hears being praised.

When she wished to avoid being caught,

The way in which she fled was where

There was a ploughman ploughing the ground,

With men in attendance. The mysterious Trinity has spoken it.

Then went the faultless mother of splendid gifts

With her happy husband. A crowd of men

Afterwards came to ask

In an entertainment,

"Hast thou seen a woman and a son with her?"

And say thou, for the record's truth,

And he will not refuse our request,

That thou didst see us going without her

To a certain spot, and the blessing of God be on it I

Upon that came a destitute rabble, a race of the disposition of Cain,

A fierce and iniquitous multitude are they;

A tower was sought, in order to seek the mysterious Being,

Then said one who was deformed and unwitty, to the man whom thou seest,-

"Host thou seen the men of the city of giants

Going by thee without turning?"

I did see them when I harrowed the fair land,

Where you see the reaping.

What the children of Cain now did, was

To turn away from the reapers.

Through the intercession of Mary Maria,

And her knowledge communicated to her by God,

There were defending them, besides herself,

The Holy Spirit and her sanctity.

Tenby

TALIESIN AE CANT {"TALIESIN sang this"}
I make a request to God, Shepherd of the people,

Ruler of heaven and earth, supreme in wisdom.

There is a fair fort upon the sea;

A splendid rise, joyful on holidays.

And when the sea is extremely turbulent,

The clamour of bards over cups of mead is customery.

Comes a swift wave toward it,

They leave the gray-green ocean to the Picts.

And may I have, O God, through my prayer,

When I may keep terms, reconciliation with thee.

There is a fair fort upon the wide water,

An impregnable fortress, surrounded by sea.

Ask, Britain, whose home is this?

O leader of the line of Ab Erbin, let it be yours!

TENBY

There was a company and there was a song

In the fortification and an eagle on high

On the path of the white-faced.

Before a splendid lord, starting up against the foe,

A warrior of widespread fame, they assembled.

There is a fair fort upon the ninth wave;

Fair its folk in resting themselves.

They do not make their pleasant life through shame;

'Tis not their custom to be stingy.

I shall not speak falsely of my welcome;

Better the captive of Dyfed than the yeoman of Deudraeth!

A host of the free in the midst of a feast;

Narrow between two of the best of people.

There is a fair fort, whose company fosters pleasure

And praise and the cry of birds.

Joy and songs on its holidays,

around a ready lord, a radiant distributor.

Before his going into an oaken chest,

he gave me mead and wine from a glass cup.

There is a fair fort on the coast;

pleasantly, each is given his share.

I know in Tenby, pure white the seagull,

the host of Bleiddudd, lord of the fort.

It was my custom on holidays,

appeasement by the bright king of battle

and a heather-coloured mantle and courtly privilege,

until I held tongue over the bards of Britain.

There is a fair fort, which abounds in song;

the freedoms I sought were mine.

I do not speak of rights: the law I kept;

he who does not know this deserves no gifts.

The writings of Britain were its chief concern,

Where the waves toss. Let it last long, the cell I visited!

There is a fair fort standing on high.

Excellent its pleasures, its praise lofty.

Fair all around it, enclosure of champions,

relentless sea-spume comes to me, far-reaching its fingers,

it explodes to the top of the rock; raucous the little sea-bird.

Anger forsworn, let it flee beyond the mountains.

And to Bleiddudd the best prosperity there may be.

I shall be burdened over beer with the task of memories.

The blessing of the lord of harmonious heaven will endure.

He who will not make us fellow-countrymen of the descendant of Owain.

There is a fair fort upon the sea-shore.

Pleasantly, each is given his desire.

Ask Gwynedd, let it be yours.

Rough, stiff spears they earned.

On Wednesday, I saw men in conflict;

on Thursday, it was reproaches they contended with.

And hair was red with blood, and lamenting on harps.

Weary were the men of Gwynedd the day they came,

and atop the stone of Maelwy they shelter shields.

A host of kinsmen fell by the descendant {of Owain?}.

Dinas Maon

DINAS MAON, MAY GOD the blessed
Sovereign defend it

What the sun will dry, Edar will moisten.

Dinas Maon, the dislike of Sovereigns,

Where kings were hewed down in the obstinate conflict.

What the sun will dry, Mervin will moisten.

Dinas Maon, the security of the country,

May the protection of God surround it!

What the sun will dry, Nynaw will moisten.

Mad put his thigh on Merchin the gray steed,

The fort of the brave will defend me.

What the sun will dry, Maelgwn will moisten.

The Birch Trees

BLESSED IS THE BIRCH in the valley of Gwy

Whose branches will fall off one by one, two by two

It will remain when there will be a battle in Ardudwy

And the lowing together of the cattle about the ford of Mochnwy

And spears and shouting at Dyganwy

And Edwin bearing sway in Mona

And youths pale and light

In ruddy clothes commanding them.

Blessed is the birch in Pumlumon

Which will see when the front of the stage shall be exalted and which will see Franks clad in mail

About the hearth food for whelps

And monks frequently riding on steeds.

Blessed is the birch in the heights of Dinwythy

Which will know when there shall be a battle in Ardudwy

And spears uplifted around Edrywy

And a bridge in the Taw, and another on the Tawy

And another, on account of a misfortun, on the banks of the Gwy

And the artificer that will make it, let his name by Garwy;

and the principle of Mona have dominion over it.

Women will be under the Gynt, and men in affliction

Happier than I is he who will welcome

The time of Cadwaladyr: a song he may sing!

The poems is often attributed to Myrddin, as one of his "prophetic" poems made during his madness in Celydon.

The Apple Trees

I Sweet appletree, your branches delight me,
Luxuriantly budding my pride and joy!
I will put before the lord of Macreu,
That on Wednesday, in the valley of Machawy
Blood will flow.
Lloegyr's (England's) blades will shine.
But hear, O little pig! on Thursday
The Cymry will rejoyce
In their defence of Cymimawd,
Furiously cutting and thrusting.
The Saesons (Saxons) will be slaughtered by our ashen spears,
And their heads used as footballs.
I prophesy the unvarnished truth -
The rising of a child in the secluded South.

II

Sweet and luxuriant appletree,

Great its branches, beautiful its form!

I predict a battle that fills me with far.

At Pengwern, men drink mead,

But around Cyminawd is a deadly hewing

By a chieftain from Eryri - til only hatred remains.

III

Sweet yellow appletree,

Growing in Tal Ardd,

I predict a battle at Prydyn,

In defense of frontiers.

Seven ships will come

Across a wide lake,

Seven hundred men come to conquer.

Of those who come, only seven will return

According to my prophecy.

IV

Sweet appletree of luxuriant growth!

I used to find food at its foot,

When because of a maid,

I slept alone in the woods of Celyddon,

Shield on shoulder, sword on ,

Hear, O little pig! listen to my

As sweet as birds that sing on Monday

When the sovereigns come across the sea,

Blessed by the Cymry (Welsh), because of their strength.

V

Sweet appletree in the glade,

Trodden is the earth around its base.

The men of Rhydderch see me not,

Gwendyyd no longer loves nor greets me

I am hated by Rhydderch's strongest scion.

I have despoiled both his son and daughter:

Death visits them all - why not me?

After Gwnddoleu no one shall honour me,

No diversions attend me,

No fair women visit me.

Though at Arderydd (Arthuret) I wore a golden torque

The swan-white woman despises me now.

VI

Sweet appletree, growing by the river,

Who will thrive on its wondrous fruit?

When my reason was intact

I used to lie at its foot

With a fair wanton maid, of slender form.

Fifty years the plaything of lawless en

I have wandered in gloom among spirits

After great wealth, and gregarious minstrels,

I have been here so long not even sprites

Can lead me astray. I never sleep, but tremble at the thought

Of my Lord Gwenddoleu, and y own native people.

Long have I suffered unease and longing--

May I be given freedom in the end.

VII

Sweet appletree, with delicate blossom,

Growing concealed, in the wind!

At the tale was told to me

That my words had offended the most powerful minister,

Not once, not twice, but thrice in a single day.

Christ! that my end has come

Before the killing of Gwndydd's son

Was upon my hands!

VIII

Sweet appletree with your delicate blossom,

Growing amid the thickets of trees!

Chwyfleian foretells,

A tale that will come to pass

A staff of gold, signifying bravery

Will be given by the glorious Dragon Kings.

The grateful one will vanquish the profaner,

Before the child, bright and bold,

The Saesons shall fall, and bards will flourish

IX

Sweet appletree of crimson colour,

Growing, concealed in the wood of Celyddon:

Though men seek your fruit, their search is vain

Until Cadwaladyr comes from Cadfaon's meeting

To Teiwi river and Tywi's lands,

Till anger and anguish come from Arawynion,

And the long-hairs are tamed.

X

Sweet appletree of crimson colour,

Growing, concealed, in the wood of Celyddon

Though men seek your fruit, their search is vain,

Till Cadwalad comes from Rhyd Rheon's meeting,

And with Cynon advances against the Saeson.

Victorious Cymry, glorious their leaden,

All shall how their rights again,

All Britons rejoice, sounding joyful horns.

Chanting songs of happiness and peace!

Listen, Piglet

LISTEN, O LITTLE PIG! happy little pig,
Do not go rooting on top of the mountain.
But stay here, secluded in the wood.
Hidden from the dogs of Rhydderch the Faithful.
I will prophecy--it will be truth!
From Aber Taradyr the Cymry will be, bound
Under one warlike leader
His name is Llywelyn, of the line of Gwynedd.
Usurpers of the Prydein he will overcome.

Listen, O little pig! we should hide
From the huntsmen of Mordei, if one dared,
Lest we be pursued and discovered.
If we escape--I'll not complain of fatigue!
I shall predict, from the back of the ninth wave,
The truth about the White One who rode Dyfed to exhaustion
Who built a church for those who only half believed,

LISTEN, PIGLET   45

In the upland region, and among wild beasts.

Until Cynan comes, nothing will be restored.

Listen, O little pig! I lack sleep,

Such a tumult of grief is within me.

Fifty years of pain I have endured.

Evil is the joy which I have now.

May life be given me by Jesus, the most trustworthy

Of the kings of heaven, of highest lineage!

It will not be well with the female decendants of Adam,

If they believe not in God, in hte latter day.

Once I saw Gwenddoleu, with the gift of Princes,

Garnering prey on every side;

Beneath my green sod is he not still!

He was the chief of the North, and the gentlest.

Listen, O little pig! it was ncessary to pray,

For fear of the five sovereigns from Normandy;

And the fifth going over the salt sea,

To conquer Iwerdon [Ireland] with its pleasant towns;

He will cause war and confusion,

And ruddy arms and groanings in it.

And they, certainly, will come from it,

And do honor on the grave of Dewi [St. David].

And I will predict that there will be confusion

From the fighting of son and father, the country shall know it;

And that there iwll be to the Lloegrians the falling of cities,

And that deliverance will never be to Normandy.

Listen, O little pig! don't sleep yet!

Rumors reach me of perjured chieftains.

And tightfisted farmers.

Soon, over the sea, shall come men in armour

On armoured horses, with destroying spears

When that happens, war will come,

Fields will be ploughed but never reaped.

Women will be cuckolds to the corpses of their men.

Mourning will come to Caer Sallawg.

Listen, O little pig! O pig of truth!

The Sybil has told me a wondrous tale.

I predict a Summer full of fury,

Between brothers, treachery from Gwynedd.

A pledge of peace will be required from Gwynedd,

Seven hundred ships from Gynt blown in by the North wind.

In Aber Dyn they will confer.

Listen, O little pig! O blessed pig!

The Sybil has told me a frightful thing

When Lloegyr encamps in the lands of Eiddyn [some texts "Ethlin"]

Making Deganwy a strong fort

By the... of Lloegyr and Llywelyn,

There will be a child on the shoulders... baggage.

When Deinoel, son of Dunawd Deinwyn, becomes enraged,

And the Franks will flee

At Aber Dulas they will fall,

Sweating in bloody garments.

Listen, O little pig! listen to the calls for attention!

For the crime of the necessitous God will make remissions.

... what is becoming, be it mine,

And what is... let him seek.

Listen, O little pig! it is broad daylight,

Hark thou to the song of water-birds whose notes are loud!

To us there will be years and long days

And iniquitous rulers, and the blasting of fruit,

And bishops sheltering theives, churches desecrated,

And monks who will compensate for loads of sins.

Listen, O little pig! go to Gwynedd.

Seek a mate when you rest.

While Rhydderch Hael feasts in his hall

He does not know what sleepless I bore

Snow to my knees, owing to the warriness of the chief

Ice in my hair, sad my fate!

Tuesday will come, the day of fierce anger

Between the rulers of Powys and Gwynedd

When the beem of light will rise from its long repose

And defend from its enemy the frontiers of Gwynedd.

Unless my Maker will grant me a share of his mercy,

Woe to inc that I have existed, miserable will be my end!

Listen, O little pig! utter not a whisper,

When the host of war marches front Carmarthen,

To support, in the common cause, two welps

Of the line of Rhys, the stay of battle, the warlike commander of armies

When the Saxon shall be slain in the conflict of Cymm erau,

Blessed will be the lot of Cyrnry, the people of Cymrwy.

Listen, O little pig! blessed little pig of the country!

Do not sleep in the morning, burrow not in the fertile region

Lest Rydderch had and his cunning dogs should come,

And before thou couldst reach the wood, thy perspiration trickled down.

Listen, O little pig! thou blessed pig!

Hadst thou seen as much severe oppression as I have,

Thou wouldst not slcep in the morning, nor burrow on the lull.

When the, Saxons repose from their serpent cunning,

And the castle of Collwyn is resorted to front afar,

Clothes will be smart, and the black pool clear.

Listen, O little pig! hear thou now

When the men of Gwynedd lay down their great work,

Blades will be in hands, horns will be sounded,

Armour will be broken before sharp lances.

And I will predict that two rightful princes

Will produce peace from heaven to earth--

Cynan, Cadwaladyr, thorough Cymry.

May their councils be admired.

The laws of the country, and the exclusion of troubles,

And the abolition of armies and theft;

And to us then there shall be a relief after our ills,

And from generosity none will be excluded.

Listen, O little pig! is not the mountain green?

My cloak is thin; for me there is no repose;

Pale is my visage; Gwendydd does not come to me.

When the men of Bryneich will bring their army to time shore,

Cymry will conquer, glorious will be their day.

Listen, O little pig! thou brawny pig!

Bury not thy snout, consume not Mynwy;

Love no pledge, love no play.

And an advice I will give to Gwenabwy,

"Be not an amorous youth given to wanton play."

And I will predict the battle of Machawy,

When there will be ruddy spears in the Riw Dydmwy,

From the contention of chieftains; breast will heave on the saddles;

There will be a morning of woe, and a woeful visitation;

A bear from Deheubarth will arise,

his men will spread over the land of Mynwy.

Blessed is the lot that awaits Gwenddydd,

When the Prince of Dyved comes to rule.

Listen, O little pig! are not the buds of thorns

Very green, time mountain beautiful, and beautiful the earth?

When two brothers will be two Idases for land,

From their claim will be cherished a lasting feud.

Listen, O little pig! to me it is of no purpose

To hear the voice of water-birds, whose scream is tumultuous,

Thin is the hair of my head, my covering is not warm;

The dales are my barn, my corn is not plenteous;

My summer collection affords me no relief,

Before parting from God, incessant was my passion.

And I will predict, before the end of the world,

Women without shame, and men without manliness.

Listen, O little pig! a trembling pig!

Thin is my covering, for me there is no repose,

Since the battle of Ardderyd it will not concern me,

Though the sky were to fall, and sea to overflow.

And I will predict that after Henri

Such and such a king in troublesome times.

When there shall be a bridge on the Taw, and another on the Tywi,

There will be an end of war in it.

The Stanzas of the Graves

THE GRAVES WHICH THE rain bedews?

Men that were not accustomed to afflict me:--

Cerwyd, and Cywryd, and Caw.

The graves which the thicket covers?

They would not succumb without avenging themselves:--

Gwryen, Moriel, and Morial.

The graves which the shower bedews?

Men that would not succumb stealthily

Gwynn, and Gwrien, and Gwriad.

The grave of Tydain, father of the Muse,[1] in the region of Bron Aren:

Where the wave makes a sullen sound

The grave of Dylan[2] in Llan Beuno.

The grave of Ceri Gledyvhir, in the region of Hen Eglwys,

In a rugged steep place

Tarw Torment in the enclosure of Corbre.

The grave of Seithenhin[3] the weak-minded

Between Caer Cenodir and the shore

Of the great sea and Cinran.

In Aber Gwenoli is the grave of Pryderi,[4]

Where the waves beat against the land

In Carrawg is the grave of Gwallawg Hir.

The grave of Gwalchmai[5] is in Peryddon,

Where the ninth wave[6] flows:

The grave of Cynon is in Llan Badarn.

The grave of Gwrwawd the honourable is

In a lofty region: in a lowly place of repose,

The grave of Cynon the son of Clydno Eiddyn.[7]

The grave of Rhun the son of Pyd is by the river Ergryd,

In a cold place in the earth.

The grave of Cynon is in Ryd Reon.

Whose is the grave beneath the hill?

The grave of a man mighty in the conflict--

The gravc of Cynon the son of Clydno Eiddyn.

The grave of the son of Osvran is in Carnlan,

After many a slaughter

The graveof Bedwyr[8] is in Gallt Tryvan.

The grave of Owain ab Urien[9] in a secluded part of the world,

Under the sod of Llan Morvael;

In Abererch, that of Rhydderch Hael.[10]

After wearing dark-brown clothes, and red, and splendid,

And riding magnificent steeds with sharp spears,

In Llan Heledd[11] is the grave of Owain.

After wounds and bloody plains,

And wearing harness and riding white horses,

This, even this, is the grave of Cynddylan.[12]

Who owns the grave of good connections?

He who would attack Lloegir[13] of the compact host--

The grave of Gwen, the son of Llywarch Hen,[14] is this.

Whose is the grave in the circular space,

Which is covered by the sea and the border of the valley?

The grave of Meigen, son of Rhun,[15] the ruler of a hundred.

Whose is the grave in the island,

Which is covered by the sea with a border of tumult?

The grave of Meigen, the son of Rhun, the ruler of a court

Narrow is the grave and long,

With respect to many long every way

The grave of Meigen, the son of Rhun, the ruler of right.

The grave of the three serene persons on an elevated hill,

In the valley of Gwynn Gwynionawg--

Mor, and Meilyr, and Madawg.

The grave of Madawg, the splendid bulwark

In the meeting of contention, the grandson of Urien,

The best son to Gwyn of Gwynlliwg.

The grave of Mor, the magnificent, immovable sovereign,

The foremost pillar in the conflict,

The son of Peredur Penwedig.[16]

The grave of Meilyr Malwynawg of a sullenly-disposed mind.

The hastener of a fortunate career,

Son to Brwyn of Brycheinawg.

Whose is the grave in Ryd Vaen Ced

With its head in a downward direction?

The grave of Rhun, the son of Alun Dywed.

The grave of Alun Dywed in his own region,

Away lie would not retreat from a difficulty--

The son of Meigen, it was well when he was born.

The grave of Llia the Gwyddel is in the retreat of Ardudwy,

Under the grass and withered leaves;

The grave of Epynt is in the vale of Gewel.

The Grave of Dywel, thc son of Erbin,[17] is in the plain of Caewaw

He would not be a vassal to a king;

Blameless, he would not shrink from battle.

The Grave of Gwrgi,[18] a hero and a Gwyndodian lion;

And the grave of Llawr, the regulator of hosts.

In the upper part of Gwanas the men are!

The long graves in Gwanas--

Their history is not had,

Whose they are and what their deeds.

There has been the family of Oeth and Anoeth[19]--

Naked are their men and their youth--

Let him who seeks for them dig in Gwanas.

The grave of Llwch Llawengin[20] is on the river Cerddenin,

The head of the Saxons of the district of Erbin;

He would not be three months without a battle.

The graves in the Long Mountain--

Multitudes well know it--

Are the graves of Gwryen, Gwryd Engwawd, and Llwyddawg the son of Lliwelydd.

Who owns the grave in the mountain?

One who marshalled armies--

It is the grave of Ffyrnvwel, the son of Hyvlydd.

Whose grave is this? The grave of Eiddiwlch the Tall,

In the upland of Pennant Twrch,

The son of Arthan, accustomed to slaughter.

The grave of Llew Llawgyffes[21] under the protection of the sea,

With which he was familiar

He was a man that never gave the truth to any one.

The grave of Beidawg the Ruddy in the vicinity of Riw Llyvnaw;

The grave of Lluosgar in Ceri;

And at Ryd Bridw the grave of Omni.

Far his turmoil and his seclusion

The sod of Machawe conceals him;

Long the lamentations for the prowess of Beidawg the Ruddy.

Far his turmoil and his fame--

The sod of Machawe is upon him--

This is Beidawg the Ruddy, the son of Einyr Llydaw.

The grave of a monarch of Prydain is in Lleudir Gwynasedd,

Where the flood enters the Llychwr;

In Celli Briafael, the grave of Gyrthmwl.

The grave in Ystyvachau,

Which everybody doubts.

The grave of Gwrtheyrn Gwrthenau.22

Clan wails in the waste of Cnud,

Yonder above the grave of the stranger--

The grave of Cynddilig, the son of Corcnud.

Truly did Elffin bring me

To try my primitive bardic lore

Over a chieftain--23

The grave of Rwvawn with the imperious aspect.

Truly did Elffin bring me

To try my bardic lore

Over an early chieftain--

The grave of Rwvawn, too early gone to the grave.

The grave of March, the grave of Gwythur;

The grave of Gwgawn Gleddyvrudd

A mystery to the world, the grave of Arthur.24

The grave of Elchwith is by the rain bedewed,

With the plain of Meweddawg under it

Cynon ought to bewail him there.

Who owns this grave? this grave? and this?

Ask me, I know it--

The grave of Ew, the grave of Eddew was this,

And the grave of Eidal with the lofty mien.

Eiddew and Eidal, the unflinching exiles,

The whelps of Cylchwydrai:

The sons of Meigen bred war-horses.

Whose is this grave? It is the grave of Brwyno the Tall,

Bold were his men in his region.

Where he would be, ther would be no flight.

Who owns this grave-not another?

Gwythiwch, the vehement in the conflict,

While he would kill thee, he would at thee laugh.

The grave of Silid the intrepid is in the locality of Edrywfy;

The grave of Lleminig25 in Llan Elwy,

In the swampy upland is the grave of Kilinwy.

The grave of a stately warrior; many a carcase

Was usual from his laud,

Before he became silent beneath the stones

Llachar, the son of Rhun, is in the valley of the Cain.

The grave of Talan Talyrth

Is at the contention of three battles,

A hewer down of the head of every force,

Liberal was lie, and open his gates.

The grave of Elisner, the son of Ner,

Is in the depth of the earth without fear, without concern

A commander of hosts was he, so long as his time lasted.

The grave of a hero vehement in his rage

Llachar the ruler of hosts, at the confluence of noisy waters,

Where the Tawne forms a wave.

Whose are graves in the fords?

What is the grave of a chieftain, the son of Rygenau,

A man whose arms had abundant success.

Whose is this grave? The grave of Braint

Between Llewin and Llednaint--

The grave of a man, the woe of his foes.

Whose is the grave on the slope of the hill?

Many who know it do not ask;

The grave of Coel, the son of Cynvelyn.26

The grave of Dehewaint is on the river Clewaint,

In the uplands of Mathavarn,

The support of mighty warriors.

The grave of Aron, the son of Dewinvin, is in the land of Gwenle;

He would not shout after thieves,

Nor disclose the truth to enemies.

The grave of Tavlogan, the son of Ludd,

Is far away in Trewrudd; and thus to us there is affliction

He who buried him obtained an advantage.

Who owns the grave on the banks of Ryddnant?

Rhun his name, his bounties were infinite

A chief he was! Rhiogan pierced him.

He was like Cyvnyssen to demand satisfaction for murder,

Ruddy was his lance, serene his aspect:

Who derived the benefit? The grave of Bradwen.

Whose is the quadrangular grave

With its four stones around the front?

The grave of Madawg the intrepid warrior.

In the soil of the region of Eivionydd,

There is a tall man of fine growth,

Who would kill all when he was greatly enraged.

The three graves on the ridge of Celvi,

Thu Awen has declared them to me

The grave of Cynon of the rugged brows,

The grave of Cynvael, and the grave of Cynveli.

The grave of Llwid Llednais in the land of Cemmaes,

Before his ribs had grown long,

The hull of conflict brought oppression thither.

The grave of the stately Siawn in Hirerw,

A mountain between the plain and the oaken forest;

Laughing, treacherous, and of bitter disposition was lie.

Who owns the grave in the sheltered place?

While he was, he was no weakling:--

It is the grave of Ebediw, the son of Maelur.

Whose is the grave in yonder woody cliff?

His hand was an enemy to many:--

The bull of battle-mercy to him!

The graves of the sea-marsh.

Slightly are they ornamented!

There is Sanawg, a stately maid;

There is Rhun, ardent in war;

There is Earwen, the daughter of Hennini;

There are Lledin and Llywy.

The grave of Hennin Henben is in the heart of Dinorben;

The grave of Aergwl in Dyved,

At the ford of Cynan Gyhored.

Every one that is not dilatory inquires--

Whose is the mausoleum that is here?

It is the grave of Einyawn, the son of Cunedda;27

It is a disgrace that in Prydain he should have been slain.

Who owns the grave in the great plain?

Proud his hand upon his lance

The grave of Beli, the son of Benlli Gawr.

NOTES:

1. Muse: lit. "Awen"--the Welsh concept of divine inspiration, similar to the Irish imbas.

2. Dylan: possibly Dylan Eil Ton (Dylan Second Wave), the twin of Lleu Llawgyffes, and son of Gwydion ap Don and Arianrhod uerch Don. His story is found in "Math vab Mathonwy," the fourth branch of the Mabinogi.

3. Seithenhin: according to "The Drowning of the Bottom Hundred" and the poem "Seithenhin", he is the individual responsible for letting the waters of Cardigan bay overtake the Cantref of Gwyddno Garanhir, drowning all the citizens.

4. Pryderi: he of the Mabinogion, which lists his grave as being "at Maen Tyryawg above Y Velen Rhyd."

5. Gwalchmai: who is better known as Sir Gawain. Thomas Malory gives his resting place as Dover Castle.

6. "the ninth wave": in Celtic myth, particularly Irish myth, the ninth wave is a symbolic boundary between this world and the Otherworld.

7. Cynon son of Clydno Eiddyn: according to some genealogies, Cynon married Morfudd uerch Urien, sister of Owain. There is a satire on him in the Lyfr Taliesin.

8. Bedwyr: Sir Bedevere

9. Owain ab Urien: Sir Yvain or Ywain of Arthurian romance. A historical prince of the sixth century who lead the Britons against the Saxons. Often mentioned by the poets of the sixth century (Taliesin particularly).

10. Rhydderch Hael: king of Strathclyde in the sixth century, contemporaneous with Urien and Owein. According to legend, he was the patron of St. Kentigern, and brother-in-law of Myrddin.

11. Llan Heledd: lit. "the Church of Heledd." What connection this has to the figure of Heledd in the Red Book poem "Canu Heledd" is unknown to me.

12. Cynddylan: warlord and brother of Heledd.

13. Lloegir: the Welsh name for England.

14. Gwen, the son of Llwyarch Hen: his name figures prominently in the poems attributed to Llwyarch. Presumably, he may have been the eldest.

15. Meigen, son of Rhun: possibly the bard who is attributed two poems in the Black Book.

16. Mor... Peredur: Mor son of Peredur is an interesting case, when one examines the story of "Sir Morien." Here, Sir Morien is a Moor who is the son of Sir Perceval. The creation of such a character may have ultimately been derived first from the Parzival of Wolfram von Eschenbach, who says that Perceval had a Muslim half-brother, while compounding that with the figure of Mor, whose name sounds like "Moor."

17. Erbin: Father of Gereint, and, I have been told, ruler of Devon.

18. Gwrgi: Usually named as brother of Peredur.

19. Oeth and Anoeth: elsewhere called the prison where Arthur was kept, until freed by his cousin Goreu ap Custennin. Iolo Morgannwg believed that it was a prison constructed of the bones of a defeated Roman legion. In truth, it is not known exactly what "Oeth and Anoeth" means, but seems to be another name for the Otherworld.

20. Llwch Llawengin: Perhaps no relation ot Llwch Lleminawg of "Culhwch and Olwen"

21. Llew Llawgyffes: he of the Mabinogion branch "Math vab Mathonwy."

22. Gwrtheyrn Gwrthenau: King Vortigern.

23. "Truly did Elffin bring me...": Does this and the following stanza represent an attempt to put this poem in the mouth of Taliesin? It does seem to reference--however obliquely--to the tradition of Taliesin besting the bards of Maelgwn.

24. "March... Arthur": March: King Mark of Tristan and Iseult. I'm not sure about the other two. Arthur of course is King Arthur. The exact words of this line: "anoeth bid bet y Arthur" are variously translated:

"A wonder of the world is the grave of Arthur"

"a difficult thing is the grave of Arthur"

"Impossible to find in this world is the grave of Arthur"

It is worth noting that the world anoeth appears, being the world "wonder" "myster" "difficult" etc. It is the name of Arthur's prison in the triads, and is reverenced a little earlier in the stanzas. What it all means, though, I can't tell you.

25. Lleminig: This is probably the Llwch Lleminawg of "Culhwch and Olwen"

26. Coel, the son of Cynvelyn: Old King Cole, and a founder of a dynastic line.

27. Cunedda: another founder of a dynastic line.

The Cynghogion of Elaeth

NOW GONE ARE MY ardour and liveliness;
If I have erred, I truly acknowledge it;
May the Lord not inflict upon me severe pain!

May not the Lord inflict severe pain
On man for his anger and passion.
A reprobate of Heaven is reprobate of earth.

Let sinful mortal believe in God,
And wake at midnight;
Let him who offends Christ sleep not.

Let not a son of man sleep for the sake of the passion
Of the Son of God, but wake up at the early dawn;
And he will obtain heaven and forgiveness.

Pardon will he obtain, who will call upon

God, and despise Him not,

And heaven the night he dies.

if a son of man dies without being reconciled

To God, for the sins which he has committed,

It is not well that a soul entered his flesh.

It is not common for the mischievous to employ himself in converse

With God, against the day of affliction,

The bold thinks that he shall not die.

Now gone —

Not To Call Upon God

NOT TO CALL UPON God, whose favour defends
Both the innocent and the angels,
Is too much of false pride;
Woe to him that does it openly in the world.

I love not treasure with traces of dwellings no longer existing;
Everything in the present state is like a summer habitation.
I am a man to Him whose praise is above all things,
To the most high God who made me.

I love to praise Peter, who can bestow true peace,
And with him his far-extending virtues;
In every language he is, with hope, acknowledged
As the gentle, high-famed, generous porter of heaven.

God I will implore to grant a request,
Lord, be Eloi my Protector!

That to my soul, for fear of torments,

Be the whole protection of all the martyrs.

Of God I will ask another request,

That my soul, to be safe from the torments. of enemies,

And held in remembrance, may have

The protection of the Virgin Mary and the holy maidens.

Of God I will ask a request also,

Just is he, and able to defend me,

That to my soul, for fear of terrible torments,

Be the protection of the Christians of the world.

Of God I will ask a considerate request,

That, being ready and diligent at all matins,

To my soul, for fear of punishment,

May be the protection of God and all the saints.

Not to call upon God —

Gereint son of Erbin

BEFORE GERAINT, THE ENEMY of oppression,
I saw white horses jaded and gory,
And after the shout, a terrible resistance.

Before Geraint, the unflinching foe,
I saw horses jaded and gory from the battle,
And after the shout, a terrible impulsion.

Before Geraint, the enemy of tyranny,
I saw horses white with foam,
And after the shout, a terrible torrent.

In Llongborth I saw the rage of slaughter,
And biers beyond all number,
And red-stained men from the assault of Geraint.

In Llongborth I saw the edges of blades in contact,

Men in terror and blood on the pate,

Before Geraint, the great son of his father.

In Llongborth I saw the spurs

Of men who would not flinch from the dread of the spears,

And the drinking of wine out of the bright glass.

In Llongborth I saw the weapons

Of men, and blood fast dropping,

And after the shout, a fearful return.

In Llongborth I saw Arthur,

And brave men who hewed down with steel,

Emperor, and conductor of the toil.

In Llongborth Geraint was slain,

A brave man from the region of Dyvnaint,

And before they were overpowered, they committed slaughter.

Under the thigh of Geraint were swift racers,

Long-legged, with wheat for their corn,

Ruddy ones, with the assault of spotted eagles.

Under the thigh of Geraint were swift racers,

Long their legs, grain was given them,

Ruddy ones, with the assault of black eagles.

Under the thigh of Geraint were swift racers,
Long-legged, restless over their grain,
Ruddy ones, with the assault of red eagles.

Under the thigh of Geraint were swift racers,
Long-legged, grain-scattering,
Ruddy ones, with the assault of white eagles.

Under the thigh of Geraint were swift racers,
Long-legged, with the pace of the stag,
With a nose like that of the consuming fire on a wild mountain.

Under the thigh of Geraint were swift racers,
Long-legged, satiated with grain,
Grey ones, with their manes tipped with silver.

Under the thigh of Geraint were swift racers,
Long-legged, well deserving of grain,
Ruddy ones, with the assault of grey eagles.

Under the thigh of Geraint were swift racers,
Long-legged, having corn for food,
Ruddy ones, with the assault of brown eagles.

When Geraint was born, open were the gates of heaven,

Christ granted what was asked,

Beautiful the appearance of glorious Prydain.

Duv in kymhorth

THIS SECTION DOES NOT have a translation in the public domain. It is included here in the original Welsh.

Duv in kymhorth in nerth in porth in canhorthuy.

Y valch teeirn dinas unbin degin adwi.

Hywel welmor. kimry oror kyghor arvy.

Terruin trochiad. torwoet ueitad vab goronvy.

Godrut y var. gurt in trydar gvae rycothvy.

Pedriauc heul. muyhaw y treul. vchel kylchwy.

Tir brycheinauc. dy iaun priaud. paup ae gwelhvy.

Nev rydadlas am luith eurgvas euas lyvuy.

Ergig anchvant. guent. gulad morgant. Dyffrin mynvy.

Gvhir penrin ystradvi brin. tywin. warvy.

Dywed dvycaun. kerediciawn. kiflaun owuy.

A meironit ac ewionit. ac ardudvy.

Ros rowynniauc. ran arderchauc. rugil yg gortuy.

Tegigil (---)al. edeirnaun ial arial arlvy.

Ryuel ebruit. a diffrin cluit. a nant convy.
Powis enwauc. a chyueilauc ac avo mvy.
Dyffrin hawren. keri dygen. kyven venvy.
Elwael buellt. maelenit guell. pell y treithvy.
Teir rac ynis. ar teir inis. ar tramordvy.
Hyuel guledic. vt gveith vutic. id y guystlvy.

Y tharkiveir ar pennic penn. o. plant nevuy.
Goruir edwin. guraul breenhin. dilywin denvy.
Dreic angerdaul turvf moroet maur. meint achupvy.
Rywiscuis llaur am y vyssaur eur amaervy.
Bei na chaned. y. tyernet anhvyet rvy.
Or saul pennaeth ageis inaeht. arvaeth camrvy.
Hydir y kymhell. hywel env opell. guell yv noc vy.
Dipryderant di yscarant. rac. y dibvy.
Dihev ittunt. trallaud kystut. achur kystvy.
Gwerin werid. gwedy clevid erid a chymvy.
Ny dav metic hid orphen bid. hid y nottvy.
Hyuel haelaf. vaur eilassaw gorescynhvy.
Caffaud hyuel urth y hoewet. wy rybuchvy.

Vy ry puched y colowin ked. clod pedrydant.
Ryuel Dywal vrien haval. arial vythein.
Guriac gueilgi dorwyn. kyvid hehowin colofyn milcant.
Llugirn deudor. lluoet agor. gur. bangor breint.

Prydus perchen priodaur ben. pen pop kinweint.

Gorev breenhin ar gollewin. hid in llundein.

Haelaw lariaw. levaf teccaf. o adaw plant.

Gwerlig haeton gvaut verdidon vaton vetveint.

Goruir menic mur gwerennic gurhid gormant.

Terruin am tir. ri reith kywir. o hil morgan.

O morccanhvc o rieinvc radev rytheint.

O teernon kywrid leon. galon reibeint

Vn vid veneid y ellyspp bid. gelleist porthant.

Heothil hir ac ew. a chein y atew trvi artuniant.

Vrten arnav. rad ac anaw. affav a phlant.

Assuynaw naut duv diamehv

T HIS SECTION DOES NOT have a translation in the public domain. It is included here in the original Welsh.

Assuynaw naut duv diamehv

Y daun aedonyauc wiffinnhev.

Ar dy guir erir aerev.

Ar dy gulad guledic dehev.

Assuinaf archaf eirchad

Ym gelwir. naut kywir kygwastad.

Ar dydrissev aer. drussad.

Ar didrissaur gvaur gwenvlad.

Assuinaw archaw arch vaur

Y periw a peris new allaur.

Naut rac dyuar car kertaur.

Ar dypirth ar diporthaur.

Assuinaf naut haut haelon

Deheuparth diheuporth kertorion.

Athturuf othtarianogion.

Athtoryf oth teern meibon.

Assuinaf y chnaut nacheluch.

Ychporth. can perthin attreguch.

Gostecwir llis gosteguch.

Gostec. beirt bart aglywuch.

Assuinaf haut naut haelvonet.

Worsset. nyth orsseiw teernet.

Ar dy torif coryf kywrisset

Ar dy teleu teilug met.

Met cuin ev gwiraud met kirn

Ae gwallav. ae gwellig in eurdirn.

Agloev y ved in edirn.

Agliv deur. aglev teeirn.

Teern weilch pridein prydaw

Ych priwgert. ych priwelod adigaw.

Ych. bart ych beirnad vytaw.

Ych porth perthin yv ataf.

Attep aganaw ar canhuyw.

Vy argluit. ergliv. wi. can dothiuf.

Lleissaun lliw llev gliv glevrit.

Laessa divar di bart wif.

Viw kertaur imruw. ruisc. morkimlaut

Gurt. ruis firt kvit kert. vahaut.

assuinasserv herv hirvlaut.

Assuinaf ar wut naw. naut.

Assuinaw naut duv diamhev. y daun.

As Long As We Sojourn

AS LONG AS WE sojourn among excess and pride,

Let our work be perfect;

Let us seek deliverance through faith,

And religion and belief, as long as there is a belief in

God through obtaining faith,

And by doing great penance daily,

Soul, why askest thou me

What my end, and will the grave be my portion?

The First Song of Yscolan

BLACK THY HORSE, BLACK thy cope,

Black thy head, black thyself,

Yes, black! art thou Yscolan?

I am Yscolan the scholar,

Slight is my clouded reason,

There is no drowning the woe of him who offends a sovereign.

For having burnt a church, and destroyed the cattle of a school,

And caused a book to be submerged,

My penance is a heavy affliction.

Creator of the creatures, of supports

The greatest, pardon me my iniquity!

He who betrayed Thee, deceived me.

A full year was given me

At Bangor on the pole of a weir;

Consider thou my suffering from sea-worms.

If I knew what I now know

As plain as the wind in the top branches of waving trees,

What I did I should never have done.

The Second Song of Yscolan

I.
The first word that I will utter

In the morning when I get up,

"May the Cross of Christ be as a vesture around me."

What belongs to my Creator I will put on

To-day, in one house will I attend.

He is not a God in whom I will not believe.

I will dress myself handsomely,

And believe in no omen which is not certain;

He that created me will strengthen me.

I have a mind to see sights,

Intending to go to sea;

May a useful purpose become a treasure!

I have a mind for an advice,

Intending to go to sea;

May the purpose be useful, Lord!

Let the raven uplift its wing,

With the intention of going far away;

May a useful purpose become better!

Let the raven uplift its wing,

With the intention of going to Rome;

May a useful purpose become glorious!

Saddle thou the bayard with the white bridle,

To course Hiraethawg with its quaking grass:

Creator of Heaven! God must be with us!

Saddle thou the bayard with the short hair,

Free in the conflict, quick in his pace;

Where the nose is, there will be snorting.

Saddle thou the bayard with the long bound,

Free in the conflict, pleasing in his pace;

The sneering of the vicious will not check the brave.

Heavy the consistence of the earth, thick leaves its cover

Bitter the drinking-horn of sweet mead;

Creator of Heaven! prosper my business!

From the progeny of the sovereign and victor,

Gwosprid, and Peter chief of every language,

Saint Ffraid, bless us on our journey!

Thou, Sun, to him intercession and vows are made,

Lord, Christ the Mysterious, the pillar of beneficence!

May I make satisfaction for my sin and actions.

II.

I asked to secular priests,

To their bishops and their judges,

"What is the best thing for the soul?"

The Paternoster, and consecrated wafers, and a holy

Creed, he who sings them for his soul,

Until the judgment will be accustomed to the best thing.

Smooth the way as thou goest, and cultivate peace,

And to thee there will be no end of mercy.

Give food to the hungry and clothes to the naked,

And say thy devotions:

From the presence of devils thou hast escaped.

The proud and the idle have pain in their flesh,

The reward of going to excess:

Beware of sifting what is not pure.

Excess of sleep, and excess of drunkenness, and too much beverage

Of mead, and too much submission to the flesh,

These are six bitter things against the judgment.

For perjury in respect of land, and the betrayment of a lord,

And the scandalising of the bounteous,

At the day of judgment let there be repentance.

By rising to matins and nocturne,

Awaking, and interceding with the saints,

Shall every Christian obtain forgiveness.

Gvledic ar bennic erbin attad

THIS SECTION DOES NOT have a translation in the public domain. It is included here in the original Welsh.

Gvledic ar bennic erbin attad.

Er barch o kyuarch. o. kyuaenad.

Ynigabil barabil ar y parad.

Vy kert ith kirpuill. kanuill kangulad.

Can vid priodaur.

Canuid meidrad maur.

Canuid kighoraru guaur goleuad.

Canuid bron proffuid. canuid inad.

Canuid riev hael. canuid. rotiad.

Canuid. athro im. namethryad.

Oth. vann. oth varan. oth virein gulad.

Nam ditaul oth. wt. vt echeiad.

Nam gwellic ymplic impled dirad.

Nam gollug oth lav. guallus trewad.

Nam ellug gan llu du digarad.

Gwledic arbennic. ban geneise.

O. honaud. nid ower traethaud imi ar a trecheis.

Nid eissev. wy kerd. kg kein ewreis.

Nid eissywed ked men y keweis.

Nid ew ym crevis dews diffleis.

Yr guneuthur. amhuill na thuill. na threis.

Nid ew duhunaur a handeneis.

Nid ew rotir new. ir neb nvy keis.

Nid rvy o awit awenyt eis.

Nid rvy o obruy a obryneis.

Nid porthi ryuic ryuegeis im born.

Nid porthi penid. ry vetyleis.

In adaud wy ren rydamvneis.

Rydid imeneid. reid ry ioles.

A Blessing To the Happy Youth

I.

A BLESSING TO THE HAPPY youth and to the fair kingdom!

Large is the wave, capacious the breast.

God is his name in the depth of every language.

Thou with energy didst overshadow the pure Mary;

Well hast Thou come in human form.

Behold here the Son of glorious hope,

Whose death proceeded from Idas.

He was, by his treachery and disgraceful conduct,

A deluder in the gentle service of his lord;

Cunning was he, but he was not wise;

And until the judgment I know not his destination.

If a bard were every poet that is

On earth, on the brine and on the cultivated plain,

On the sand and on the seas, and in the stars of astronomy,

The giver with the gentle and ready hand being judge,

More than they could I should wish, and also do,

To relate the power and bounty of the Creator.

Great God! to-day is thy majesty extolled.

II.

The blessing of the nine hosts of heaven on the mysterious

Creator, the mighty God and dominator,

Who has created the light of gladness,

And generous brightness of the sun in the day,

Like the Christian's lamp, it shines above the deep,

A thousand times greater than the moon.

And a third wonder is, the agitation of the sea;

how it ebbs, how it swells,

How it goes, how it comes, how it rolls, how it settles;

How long will it go, or how will it be?

At the end of seven years,

The Creator will check its course,

Until it comes to its former state.

We will worship him who causes it, the mighty

God, the Son of Mary, who created heaven and earth.

When thou camest on Easter eve

From Uffern, what was thy portion became liberated;

Creator of heaven! may we purchase thy loving-kindness!

Keen the Gale

KEEN IS THE GALE, hare the hill,
It is difficult to find a shelter;
The ford is turbid, frozen is the lake,
A man stands firm with one stalk.

Wave after wave rolls towards the shore;
Loud the shoutings in front of the heights of the hill,
If one but just stands out.

Cold is the place of the lake before the winter storm
Dry the stalks of broken reeds;
Lucky is he who sees the wood in the chest.

Cold is the bed of fish in the shelter of a sheet of ice;
Lean the stag; the topmost reeds move quickly;
Short the evening; bent the trees.

Let the white snow fall in deposits;
Warriors will not leave their duty;
Cold are the lakes without the appearance of warmth.

Let the white snow fall on the hoar frost;
Idle is the shield on the shoulder of the aged;
The wind is very high; it has certainly frozen.

Let the snow fall on the surface of the ice;
Gently sweeps the wind the tops of thick trees;
Firm is the shield on the shoulder of the brave.

Let the snow descend and cover the vale
Warriors will hasten to battle
I shall not go;--infirmity will not let me

Let the snow fall from the side of the slope;
Prisoner is the steed, lean the cattle;
Cold is no pleasure to-day.

Lot the snow fall; white is the mountain-region
Bare the timber of the ship on sea;
A host of men will cherish many counsels.

Golden hands around the horns, the horns in agitation;

KEEN THE GALE

Cold the stream, bright the sky,

Short the evening, bending arc the tops of trees.

The bees (live) on their store; small the clamour of birds,

The day is dewless;

The hill-top is a conspicuous object; red the dawn.

The bees are under cover; cold also is the ford,

Let the frost freeze as long as it lasts:

To him that is soft may dissolution happen!

The bees are in confinement this very day;

How withered the stalks, hard the slope;

Cold and dewless is the earth to-day.

The bees are in shelter from the wet of winter;

Blue the mist, hollow tire cow-parsnip;

Cowardliness is a bad quality in a man.

Long the night, bare the moor, hoary the cliff;

Gray the fair gull on the precipice;

Bough the seas ; there will be rain to-day.

Dry the wind, wet the road,

The vale assumes its former appearance.

Cold the thistle-stalks; lean the stag;
Smooth the river; there will no fine weather

Foul the weather on the mountain; the rivers troubled
Flood will wet the ground in towns;
The earth looks like the ocean!

Thou art not a scholar, thou art not a recluse;
Thou wilt not be called a monarch in the day of necessity.
Alas! Cynddilig, that thou wert not a woman!

Let the crooked hart bound at the top of the sheltered vale;
May the ice be broken; bare are the lowlands;
The brave escapes from many a hardship.

The thrush has a spotted breast,
Spotted the breast of the thrush;
The edge of the bank is broken
By the hoof of the lean, crooked, and stooping bent.

Very high is the loud-sounding wind;
It is scarcely right for one to stand out.

At All-Saints it is habitual for the heath-tops to be dun;

High-foaming is the sea-wave,

Short the day :-Druid, your advice!

If the shield, and the vigour of the steed,

And of brave, fearless men, have gone to sleep,

The night is fair to chase the foe.

The wind is supreme; sere and bare the trees,

Withered the reeds; the hart is bounding;

Pelis the False, what land is this?

If it poured down snow as far as Arvwl Melyn,

Gloom would not make mc sad;

I would lead a host to the hill of Tydw.

For thou knowest, with equal ease, the causeway,

The ford, and the ascent, if snow were to fall,

When thou, Pelis, art our guide.

Anxiety in Prydain will not cause me to-night

To march upon a region where there is the greatest wailing,

From following after Owain.

Since thou bearest arms and shield upon thee,

Defender of the destructive battle,

Pelis, in what land wast thou fostered?

The man whom God releases from a very close prison,
Ruddy will be his spear from the territory of Owain,
Lavish of his entertainments.

Since the chieftain is gone to earth,
Pursue not his family;
After mead seek no disgrace.

The morning with the dawn of day,
When Mwg Mawr Drefydd was assaulted,
The steeds of Mechydd were not trained up.

Joy will be to be of no benefit,
Owing to the news which apprises me
That a wooden cover is upon Mechydd!

They met around Cavall;
A corpse is there in blood through injustice,
From the encounter of Rhun and the other hero.

For the staffiers of Mwg have slain Mechydd;
Drudwas did not perceive the day;
Creator of heaven! thou last caused me severe affliction!

Men are in the shout (of war); the ford is frozen over;

Cold the wave, variegated the bosom of the sea;

The eternal God give us counsel!

Mechydd, the son of Llywarch, the undaunted chief,

Fine and fair was his robe of the colour of the swan,

The first that fastened a horse by the bridle.

Arthur and the Porter

WHAT MAN IS THE porter?

Glewlwyd Gavaelvawr.[1]

Who is the man that asks it?

Arthur and the fair Cai.

How goes it with thee?

Truly in the best way in the world.

Into my house thou shalt not come,

Unless thou prevailest.

I forbid it.

Thou shalt see it.

If Wythnaint were to go,

The three would be unlucky

Mabon, the son of Modron,[2]

The servant of Uthyr Pendragon;

Cysgaint, the son of Banon;

And Gwyn Godybrion.

Terrible were my servants

Defending their rights.

Manawydan, the son of Llyr,

Deep was his counsel.

Did not Manawyd bring

Perforated shields from Trywruid?

And Mabon, the son of Mellt,

Spotted the grass with blood?

And Anwas Adeiniog,

And Llwch Llawynnog--Guardians were they

On Eiddyn Cymminog,

A chieftain that patronised them.

He would have his will and make redress.

Cai entreated him,

While he killed every third person.

When Celli was lost,

Cuelli was found; and rejoiced

Cai, as long as he hewed down.

Arthur distributed gifts,

The blood trickled down.

In the hail of Awarnach,

Fighting with a hag,

He cleft the head of Paiach.

In the fastnesses of Dissethach,

In Mynyd Eiddyn,

He contended with Cynvyn;

By the hundred there they fell,

There they fell by the hundred,

Before the accomplished Bedwyr.

On the strands of Trywruid,

Contending with Garwlwyd,

Brave was his disposition,

With sword and shield;

Vanity were the foremost men

Compared with Cai in the battle.

The sword in the battle

Was unerring in his hand.

They were stanch commanders

Of a legion for the benefit of the country- Bedwyr and Bridlaw;

Nine hundred would to them listen;

Six hundred gasping for breath

Would be the cost of attacking them.

Servants I have had,

Better it was when they were.

Before the chiefs of Emrais

I saw Cai in haste.

Booty for chieftains

Was Gwrhir among foes;

Heavy was his vengeance,

Severe his advance.

When he drank from the horn,

He would drink with four.

To battle when he would come

By the hundred would he slaughter;

There was no day that would satisfy him.

Unmerited was the death of Cai.

Cai the fair, and Llachau,3

Battles did they sustain,

Before the pang of blue shafts.

In the heights of Ystavingon

Cai pierced nine witches.

Cai the fair went to Mona,

To devastate Llewon.

His shield was ready

Against Oath Palug

When the people welcomed him.

Who pierced the Cath Palug?

Nine score before dawn

Would fall for its food.

Nine score chieftains...

[here the manuscript breaks off]

1. Glewlwyd Gavaelvawr: "Glwelwyd Mighty-grasp" goes on to become Arthur's porter, as seen in the three romances, plus "Culhwch" and "Rhonabwy"

2. Mabon: who is the prisoner to be released from Caer Llowy (Gloucester) in "Culhwch"

3. Cai... and Llachau: In Y Seint Greal (the Welsh version of Perlesvaus: The High History of the Holy Grail), Cai kills Llachau out of envy for the younger man's prowess (moreover, Llachau was Arthur's son and presumed heir; killing him paved the way for Mordred).

The poem is a dialogue between Arthur--who seems not a king but the leader of a war band--and Glewlwyd; in fact, it parallels Culhwch's attempt to enter Arthur's court, with the listing of Arthur's warriors.

A Song on Gwallawg ab Llenawg

ON A FINE NIGHT Pen Gethin heard the shout of a host,

When he took a long leap;

Unless the ground be guarded he will not cease.

Since Coegawg is so rich as this in gold,

Close to the court of Gwallawg,

I also shall be wealthy.

Accursed be the tree

Which pulled out his eye in his presence,

Gwallawg ab Lleenawg, the ruler.

Accursed be the black tree

That pulled out his eye from its place,

Gwallawg ab Lleenawg, the chief of armies.

Accursed be the white tree

That pulled out his eye from his head,

Gwallawg ab Lleenawg, the sovereign.

Accursed be the green tree

That pulled out his eye when a youth,

Gwallawg ab Lleenawg, the honourable.[1]

1. In the margins is are these two verses:

No one that was eminent went

In the way that Gwallawg did,

With his steel into the meadow.

No one that was honourable went

In the way that Meurig did,

With a bandage to the woman in three folds.

The Dialogue of Gwyn ap Nudd and Gwyddno Garahir

BULL OF CONFLICT WAS he, active in dispersing an arrayed army,

The ruler of hosts, Indisposed to anger,

Blameless and pure his conduct in protecting life.

Against a hero stout was his advance,

The ruler of hosts, disposer of wrath.

There will be protection for thee since thou askest it.

For thou hast given me protection;

How warmly wert thou welcomed!

The hero of hosts, from what region thou comest?

I come from battle and conflict

With a shield in my hand;

Broken is the helmet by the pushing of spears.

I will address thee, exalted man,

With his shield in distress;

Brave man, what is thy descent?

Hound-hoofed is my horse, the torment of battle,

Whilst I am called Gwyn, the son of Nud,

The lover of Creudilad, the daughter of Llud.

Since it is thou, Gwyn, an upright mau,

From thee there is no concealing;

I also am Gwydneu Garanhir.

He will not leave me in a parley with thee,

By the bridle, as is becoming;

But will hasten away to his home on the Tawy.

It is not the nearest Tawy I speak of to thee,

But the furthest Tawy

Eagle! I will cause the furious sea to ebb.

Polished is my ring, golden my saddle and bright

To my sadness

I saw a conflict before Caer Vandwy.

Before Caer Vandwy a host I saw,

Shields were shattered and ribs broken

Renowned and splendid was he who made the assault.

Gwyn ab Nud, the hope of armies,

Sooner would legions fall before the hoofs

Of thy horses, than broken rushes to the ground.

handsome my dog and round-bodied,

And truly the best of dogs;

Dormach was he, which belonged to Maelgwn.

Dormach with the ruddy nose! what a gazer

Thou art upon me! because I notice

Thy wanderings on Gwibir Vynyd.

I have been in the place where was killed Gwendoleu,

The son of Ceidaw, the pillar of songs,

When the ravens screamed over blood.

I have been in the place where Bran was killed,

The son of Gweryd, of far-extending fame,

When the ravens of the battle-field screamed.

I have been where Llachau was slain,

The son of Arthur, extolled in songs,

When the ravens screamed over blood.

I have been where Meurig was killed,

The son of Carreian, of hdnourable fame,

When the ravens screamed over flesh.

1 have not (?) been where Gwallawg was killed,

The son of Goholeth, the accomplished,

The resister of Lloegir, the son of Lleynawg.

I have been where the soldiers of Prydain were slain,

From the East to the North;

I am alive, they in their graves!

I have been where the soldiers of Prydain were slain,

From the East to the South

I am alive, they in death!

Though I Love the Strand

THOUGH I LOVE THE strand, I hate the sea.

How the wave covered the stone of Camwr!

The brave, the magnanimous, the amiable, the generous, and the energetic,

Are as stepping-stones to the bards of the world, and are advantageous shelter.

The fame of Heilyn proved a benefit to the solicitous.

To the day of judgment may his celebrity remain!

Though I love the strand, I hate the wave.

The wave has done violence, dismal the blow to the breast.

He will complain as long as he believes on its account.

It is a cheerful work to bathe on my bosom,

Though it (the water) fills the cavity, it does not disturb the heart.

And in the direction of Cyhaig did time wave arise.

Sorry we are for his concerns,

When Pebrwr from afar hastened to his death.

The brave and courageous multitude will affect us both

As the water hearing the leaves shows it thee.

Mechydd is sad on account of thy coming.

I will not receive thee to my receptacle.

From my part I sold a horse for thee.

Cyhaig will revenge for the delay of his enjoyment,

And for the sweet strains.

O dwarf! for thy anger to me there have been enemies.

The Dialogue of Taliesin and Ugnach

Taliesin:

A HORSEMAN resorts to the city,

With his white dogs, and large horns;

I, who have not before seen thee, know thee not.

Ugnach:

A horseman resorts to the river's mouth,

On a stout and warlike steed;

Come with me, let me not be refused.

Taliesin:

I will not go that way at present;

Bear with the conduct of the delayer;

And may the blessing of heaven and earth come (upon thee).

Ugnach:

Thou, who hast not seen me daily,

And who resemblest a prudent man,

How long wilt thou absent thyself and when wilt thou come?

Taliesin:

When I return from Caer Seon [Jerusalem? Seon > Sion > Zion?],

From contending with Jews,

I will come to the city of Lleu and Gwydion.

Ugnach:

Come with me into the city,

Thou shalt have wine which I have set apart,

And pure gold on thy clasp.

Taliesin:

I know not the confident man,

Who owns a lire and a couch;

Fairly and sweetly dost thou speak.

Ugnach:

Come with me to my dwelling,

Thou shalt have high foaming wine.

My name is Ugnach, the son of Mydno.

Taliesin:

Ugnach a blessing on thy throne!

And mnayst thou have grace and honour!

I am Taliessin who will repay thee thy banquet.

Marunad Madawc mad Maredut

THIS SECTION DOES NOT have a translation in the public domain. It is included here in the original Welsh.

Marunad Madawc mab Maredut.

Kyntelv Pridit Mawr Ae Cant.

Goduryw o glyuaw. ar claur

Maelenit. mur eluit eluan gaur.

Teulv Madauc mad anhaur.

Mal teulv. bann benlli gaur.

Goduryw a glyaw. ar claur ieithon.

Hir. hydir y wir ar saesson.

Teulv madawc mur galon.

Mal turuw. tormenhoet kinon.

Goduryw a glivaw. godor drein

Waewaur guae loegir in dit kein.

Teulv madauc mur prydein.

Yn lluithauc. in llithiav brein.

Goduryw a gliuaw. ar claur llavur.

Rei. ryuelclod dissegur.

Teulv madauc mur eglur.

Mal gavr toryw tenlu arthur.

Goduryw a glyaw. ar claur vagv

Glyv. gloev madauc byeiwu.

Trinva kyva kinytu.

Trydit tri diweir teulv.

Marunad Madawc fil Maredut

THIS SECTION DOES NOT have a translation in the public domain. It is included here in the original Welsh.

Kywarchaw im ri. rad wobeith

Kywarchaw kywercheise canweith.

Y prowi prydv. opriwieth.

Eurgert. ym argluit kedymteith.

Y cvinav madauc. metweith

Y alar. ae alon ympob ieith.

Dor yscor iscvid canhimteith.

Tarian in aerwan. in evrweith.

Turuw gruc yg gotuc goteith.

Tariw escar y iscuid in dileith.

Rwy mirt kyrt kertorion. wobeith.

Rut dilut diletyw kedimteith.

Ry gelwid. madauc. kin noe leith.

Ruid galon. y. vogion diffeith.

Rvit attaw attep vygobeith.

Rit. wisscoet. wessgvin canhimteith.

Rut on gir. Bran vab llir lledieith.

Ruit y clod includav anreith.

Rut woauc vaon ny oleith.

Rad wastad gwistlon canhimteith.

Llawin aryrad. ig kad ig cvnlleith.*

Llav escud. dan iscvd calchwreith.

Llev powis peues diobeith.

Haul owin. gur ny minn mabweith.

Hvil yscvn yscvid pedeirieith.**

Hael madauc. veuder anhyweith.

Can deryv. darfv am oeleith.

Can daeraud. darw kedymteith.

Oet beirtcar. bart clvm di ledieith

Oet cadarn agor. dywinmor diffeith.

Oet hir y truited. oed hyged higar.

Oet llawar guyar. oe kywarweith.

Oet buelin blas. gwanas gwadreith,

Oet eurllev. o aer llin kadieith.

Oet diwarn kadarn kedymteith unbin.

Oet dirn in heirn. haearn y talheith.

Ae diwet yspo. canbv. y leith.

Ydiwin y cam kymeint y affeith.

Yg goleuder seint. ig goleudeith.

Yg goleuad rad. ridid perfeith.

* in the margin: Llawin gviar a gar. o kidweith

** in the margin: Hil teirn in herin henveith

Seithenhin

SEITHENHIN, STAND THOU FORTH,
AND behold hte billowy rows;

The sea has covered the plain of Gwydneu.

Accursed be the damsel,

Who, after the wailing,

Let loose the Fountain of Venus, the raging deep.

Accursed be the maiden,

Who, after the conflict, let loose

The fountain of Venus, the desolating sea.

A great cry from the roaring sea arises above the summit of the rampart,

To-day even to God does the supplication come!

Common after excess there ensues restraint.

A cry from the roaring sea overpowers me this night,

And it is not easy to relieve me;

Common after excess succeeds adversity.

A cry from the roaring sea comes upon the winds;

The mighty and beneficent God has caused it!

Common after excess is want.

A cry from the roaring sea

Impels me from my resting-place this night;

Common after excess is far-extending destruction.

The grave of Seithenhin the weak-minded

Between Caer Cenedir and the shore

Of the great sea and Cinran.

The Names of the Sons of Llywarch Hen

SWEETLY SINGS THE BIRD on the fragrant tree
Over the head of Gwen; before his covering over with sod,
He used to fracture the armour of (Llywarch) Hen.

The three best men in their country,
To defend their homesteads,-
Eithir, and Erthir, and Argad.

The three sons of Llywarch, three intractable ones in battle.
Three fierce contenders,-
Llew, and Araw, and Urien.

Better may it be for my concerns,
That he be left on the banks of the river,
With a host of warlike men.

The bull of conflict, conductor of the war,

The support of battle, and the lamp of benevolence,
Father of heaven, increase Thou his energy!

The best three men under heaven
To defend their homes,
Pyll, and Selyv, and Sandev.

The morning with the dawn of day,
When Mwg Mawr Drefydd was assaulted,
The steeds of Mechydd were not trained up.

They mmmct around Cavall;
A corpse is there in blood through injustice,
From the rencounter of Rhun and the other hero.

A shout will be uttered on the top of Mount Llug
Over the grave of Cynllug;
The reproach is mine; it was I that caused it.

Let time snow descend and cover time vale,
Warriors will hasten to battle;
I do not go; infirmity leaves me not.

Thou art not a scholar, thou art not a recluse;
Thou wilt not be called a monarch in time day of necessity;

Alas! Cynddilig, that thou wed not a woman.

Far away is Aber Llyw,

Further are the two Cyvedlyws;

Talan, this day thou hast paid me with tears.

More Celtic Legends

We'd love for you to join our community! For more Celtic texts, resources, and fiction, visit some of the links below!

The Website

www.mythbank.com

Facebook

www.facebook.com/mythbank

Instagram

instagram.com/mythbankwebsite

Printed in Great Britain
by Amazon